PUFFIN BOOKS

The Golden Key

Dan Lee spends his time travelling between Asia and Britain. A wing chun master, he also trains in kickboxing and ju-jitsu.

TANGSHAN TIGERS

The Golden Key

Dan Lee

PUFFIN

W .... *obshaw*

PUFFIN BOOKS

Published by the Penguin Group
Penguin Books Ltd, 80 Strand, London WC2R ORL, England
Penguin Group (USA) Inc., 375 Hudson Street, New York, New York 10014, USA
Penguin Group (Canada), 90 Eglinton Avenue East, Suite 700, Toronto, Ontario, Canada M4P 2Y3
(a division of Pearson Penguin Canada Inc.)
Penguin Ireland, 25 St Stephen's Green, Dublin 2, Ireland (a division of Penguin Books Ltd)
Penguin Group (Australia), 250 Camberwell Road, Camberwell, Victoria 3124, Australia
(a division of Pearson Australia Group Pty Ltd)
Penguin Books India Pvt Ltd, 11 Community Centre, Panchsheel Park,
New Delhi – 110 017, India
Penguin Group (NZ), 67 Apollo Drive, Rosedale, North Shore 0632, New Zealand
(a division of Pearson New Zealand Ltd)
Penguin Books (South Africa) (Pty) Ltd, 24 Sturdee Avenue, Rosebank,
Johannesburg 2196, South Africa

Penguin Books Ltd, Registered Offices: 80 Strand, London WC2R ORL, England

puffinbooks.co.uk

Published 2008
1

Series created by Working Partners Ltd, London
Text copyright © Working Partners Ltd, 2008
All rights reserved

The moral right of the author has been asserted

Set in Bembo
Typeset by Palimpsest Book Production Limited, Grangemouth, Stirlingshire
Made and printed in England by Clays Ltd, St Ives plc

British Library Cataloguing in Publication Data
A CIP catalogue record for this book is available from the British Library

ISBN: 978-0-141-32284-1

CONTENTS

THE HUMAN PYRAMID

Matt faced his opponent. The other boy was tall and tough-looking, dressed in the black martial arts suit of the Shanghai Academy. He eyeballed Matt and said softly, barely moving his lips, 'You're dead, kid.'

Matt said nothing, though he narrowed his eyes meaningfully.

They bowed. The fight began.

His opponent threw rapid straight-armed punches. Matt blocked the first two, but the third came in under his guard and thudded

I

into his ribs. Matt stepped back, half-turned and launched a reverse kick that hit his opponent in the chest. The other boy grunted, gave ground, then came in again with a low side-kick that took Matt on the knee, making him stagger. His opponent was throwing everything at him, a whirlwind of high kicks and spear-hand punches. One crashed into his shoulder, making him wince. The crowd were on their feet, filling the hall with their excited roar.

Matt defended himself as best he could. He knew he had been outscored so far in the bout, and he was running out of time to strike back for the Beijing team . . .

Suddenly he saw his opportunity. His opponent had left himself open in his furious attack. Fast as a striking snake, Matt swung a roundhouse kick that hit his opponent squarely in the jaw. His opponent staggered back, winded, but still on his feet. He was there for the taking – one more well-placed kick, and Matt could win the bout.

An earsplitting bell cut through the roar of the crowd. *What does that mean?* Matt wondered. Was it the end of the contest? Had he done enough to win it?

He turned to look at the judges' table, but their faces were impassive.

The bell went on and on. It seemed to be right inside Matt's head . . .

He opened his eyes. The early morning sunlight was streaming in through the window. On the bedside table, his alarm clock rang shrilly. Matt slapped it off and sat up.

'Hey, Matt!' It was the voice of Johnny Goldberg, his friend and room-mate. He stood by the floor-to-ceiling window. Behind him, the sun glinted on the skyscrapers of Beijing.

3

'That must have been some dream you were having!' he said.

'Yeah,' said Matt. 'I was dreaming about yesterday's tournament.'

Johnny grinned. 'Wasn't it cool?'

'Well cool,' said Matt. Johnny didn't know just *how* cool yesterday had been. Not only had the Beijing Academy won the martial arts tournament against the Shanghai Academy, but the Tangshan Tigers – himself, Shawn Hung, Olivier Girard and Catarina Ribeiro – had cracked their first case. The original Tangshan Tigers had been a legendary elite fighting team, who followed a strict code of secrecy. Matt and his friends had agreed it was safest to uphold this code of honour. They couldn't tell anyone in the Academy about their gang. Not even Johnny, as much as Matt wanted to.

They had needed help from elsewhere, though. Li-Lian, a Chinese girl, had helped them solve the mystery of the Jade Dish. *We ought to find her again*, Matt thought, as he kicked the quilt off himself. To thank her, and tell her what had happened. Maybe they should –

'You'd better get a move on,' called Johnny, from the bathroom. 'Even tournament winners still have lessons. You've a training session with Master Chang before breakfast, remember?'

'Oh, yeah,' yawned Matt. He swung his legs out of bed. He felt a sharp ache in his shoulder from where he'd been thrown yesterday. But he didn't mind. It was a souvenir of his victory.

He padded into the en suite bathroom to take a shower, wondering what Chang had in store for them this morning.

Chang Sifu, or Master Chang, was waiting for them in the training hall, or *kwoon*, as Matt had learned to call it. As usual, Chang wore a plain white kung fu suit with a black silk sash. He stood with his feet slightly apart, relaxed yet very straight, radiating an air of calm authority. The eleven squad members gathered around him in a semi-circle.

Matt stood next to the other Tangshan Tigers – Chinese-American Shawn, Olivier, the handsome Swiss boy, and the Brazilian girl, Catarina, tall and slender, with her dark hair tied back in a ponytail. Each of them exchanged sly winks and grins. He wanted to tell them his idea about Li-Lian, as soon as they got a moment to themselves. But there was no time now – Master Chang was speaking.

'First,' said Chang quietly, 'let me congratulate you on yesterday's victory.'

'Yeah!' shouted Catarina, punching the air. 'All right!' At once the *kwoon* was filled with cheers as the squad celebrated. Matt joined in, feeling pleased and proud, exchanging high fives with everyone around him. Shawn hollered as if he was at a football match. Matt looked back at Chang, and saw him watching them with a patient half-smile. When the noise died down, Chang said: 'But even champions must keep training. *Especially* champions. In today's session we practise –'

He was interrupted as the door opened and in came Mr Wu, the Principal. He wore a smart grey suit and a tie with a jewelled tie-pin, and he was beaming.

'A splendid victory yesterday!' he announced. 'You were a great credit to my school! Beijing International Academy is top dog once again, and that is as it should be!' He went round all of the team, shaking hands and slapping backs. 'We showed those Shanghai pupils a thing or two, did we not?' He beamed around at them all once again. 'Well, Master

Chang, do not let me stop your excellent work – we want to be sure that our next opponents will be crushed too! I shall see you all at the Official Presentation Ceremony in the Great Hall at noon today. Carry on, Master Chang!'

Chang bowed slightly. Mr Wu trotted out, the heels of his shiny black shoes clicking over the floor. Matt wasn't sure why, but Mr Wu's bragging made him feel a little less proud of the squad's achievement – he preferred Chang's quiet dignity.

'We begin with activity to empty your heads of victory,' Chang said. 'You have enjoyed it, and that is natural, but now it is time to move on. Do not dwell on past glories. They mean nothing when next challenge comes along. Everyone please to sit.'

They sat cross-legged on the mat. In the centre, Chang placed a shallow basin of water in which floated a pinkish-white flower.

'This is lotus,' Chang explained. 'A simple meditation practice. Study lotus carefully, and when you are ready, close your eyes and keep a clear image of it in your mind.'

'Oh, terrific,' grumbled Carl Warrick. 'What is this, a botany class? That'll really help us win tournaments, won't it, thinking about flowers –'

'Carl,' said Chang gently, 'you take long time to learn. You doubted usefulness of my techniques before last tournament – but I think you must agree they were of some help to you there. Be more open-minded; you will learn better. Remember, the strong man accepts help; the weak man struggles on alone.'

Carl said nothing, but stared sullenly at the floor.

'Focus on lotus,' said Chang softly. 'Clear minds of all else for ten minutes.'

Matt closed his eyes and let the image of the

pinkish-white flower hover in the dark. Stray thoughts popped into his mind – memories of the tournament, of the Emperor's Jade Dish, of his old school back in London – but each time he pushed them away and concentrated on the lotus. He was aware of his breathing slowing down. He began to feel relaxed – detached – almost as if he was floating . . .

He was amazed when Chang gently clapped his hands. Had ten minutes passed already? His mind felt clear and refreshed.

'Slowly come back to surface,' said Chang. 'Open your eyes when ready . . . Now, work in pairs, please. Find a partner – there are eleven of you, so we will need one group of three. Yes, Matt, Shawn and Catarina. Observe these movements.' He performed a simple series of actions: stepping forward two paces, pushing forward with both hands, then repeating it in reverse, stepping backwards. He did it very slowly and rhythmically, as if performing some ancient dance. 'Do this in your pairs. As one partner goes forward, the other partner goes backwards. Maintain a rhythm, and do not be distracted by anything you see or hear.'

Matt began the movements, facing Shawn and Catarina. They soon fell into a steady rhythm, backwards, forward, backwards, forward. *It's like pushing a swing and seeing it come back to you*, thought Matt.

Suddenly there was a loud banging sound, followed by several more bangs, in an irregular rhythm. Matt jumped slightly. Chang was walking around beating on a hand-drum. What on earth . . .? Then Matt realized that this was all part of the exercise. Chang was trying to distract them. Matt banished the noise from his mind and concentrated on the movements.

The banging stopped. Chang came on to the mat and Matt saw him walk softly up to Carl and his partner Wolfgang until he was standing so close to them he was almost touching, staring at them without speaking.

Carl spun round. 'What?' he said.

'You must maintain rhythm, Carl.'

'I was! It was you who distracted me!'

'You must ignore distraction.'

Carl flushed with anger, muttering under his breath as Master Chang moved away. When Chang came and stood close to Catarina she let out a snort of laughter. Several other students started laughing too. The laughter was infectious. Matt found it really difficult to keep his face straight when Chang loomed up before him. He felt his mouth twitching as laughter welled up inside him. He bit his lip and forced himself to concentrate on the rhythm of the movements. Step, step, push, step, step, push . . .

Chang clapped his hands. 'And rest. Some of

you found this exercise difficult, but it teaches essential skills for a martial artist – how to stay calm and level-headed at all times. Be aware of what is happening all around you, but do not let it influence or cloud judgement. This is useful preparation for main task of this session.'

'Yeah, and what's that?' muttered Carl. 'Playing ring-a-ring o' roses, or –'

'No, Carl,' said Chang serenely. 'Building a human pyramid.'

A human pyramid! Matt felt a stab of excitement.

'A what?' chorused several students.

'Training exercise to build confidence, concentration, strength, balance – and trust,' explained Chang.

It sounded crazy – but there was always a good reason behind Chang's crazy ideas. Shawn glanced at him, raised his eyebrows and smiled.

13

Matt could tell Shawn was thinking the same thing.

'How are we going to build a human pyramid, sir?' asked Catarina.

'I will leave that up to you,' said Chang. 'Organize yourselves, please.'

Chang Sifu retired to the edge of the mat and stood watching them.

There was a moment's silence, then everyone started talking at once.

'Wait,' said Matt. 'We need to work together on this. We could do it with four tiers, right? Five at the bottom, then three above that, then two, then one at the top. Lola's the smallest, so she should go at the top.'

The Nigerian girl, Lola, giggled. 'Sure, why not?'

'But who's going at the bottom?' asked Olivier.

'That should be the biggest ones, I guess,'

said Matt. 'So that would be you, Olivier, and Stephane and Dani and Carl and me.'

'Hey, what about me?' said Catarina. 'I'm the tallest one here!'

'Yeah, but you're lighter than us. You should go on our shoulders, with Wolfgang and Abdul. Then Claire and Shawn go on the third tier. Then Lola right at the top.'

'Like a fairy on a Christmas tree!' said Claire, and everyone laughed.

'OK,' said Matt. 'Let's go!'

He, Olivier, Carl, Stephane and Dani formed a circle in the centre of the mat, arms round each other's shoulders.

'Ready?' asked Matt.

'Ready!' said Catarina. She made a running jump and hoisted herself up, planting one bare foot on Matt's shoulder and one bare foot on Olivier's. Matt swayed and regained his balance, adjusting to the weight. That wasn't too bad,

15

but when Wolfgang and Abdul climbed up too, the balance shifted again. Matt felt the whole circle shifting sideways, and had no choice but to go with it. They stumbled across the mat.

'Hey, stand still, you guys!' said Olivier.

'I'm trying to stand still!' grumbled Carl. 'It's you guys – you keep moving!'

They recovered themselves, but it was difficult staying stable.

'OK,' panted Matt. 'Ready for the next tier?'

He managed to free one hand and held it out so that Claire could grasp it and climb up. Claire got her knee on to Matt's shoulder, dislodging Catarina's foot in the process.

'Hey, watch out!' shouted Catarina.

'Sorry!' said Claire, as she hauled herself up, inadvertently pushing her foot into Matt's face. Matt staggered as Catarina above him moved to make room for Claire. Meanwhile,

Shawn was climbing up on the other side, and was perched precariously, on his knees, on the shoulders of Carl and Stephane, grabbing on to Wolfgang's tunic.

'Watch out, you'll pull me down!' said Wolfgang.

'Ow!' said Carl. 'This is stupid! If I wanted to spend my time doing this I'd run away and join a circus!'

'Don't talk!' Catarina told him. 'Concentrate!'

'What about you? You're talking!' Carl fired back.

'Yeah, but only to tell you to shut up!' said Catarina.

'Maybe you should try shutting up yourself!'

The task was hard enough as it was, but Matt realized this bickering was making things worse. They had to work together if they were to have a chance of succeeding. The combined

17

weight of Catarina and Claire was now pushing down on Matt, more heavily on his right side than his left. This made him stagger to the right, trying to regain balance; meanwhile, the other side of the circle was moving in the opposite direction. They couldn't hold it – the circle was falling apart!

There was a second or two of desperate, confused movement – and then the whole structure tottered and collapsed like a falling tower of Jenga.

Matt crawled out from underneath Catarina. He wasn't hurt, but frustrated at their failure to complete the task. From the expressions on his classmates' faces, everyone else felt the same way.

'This is impossible!' Catarina declared. 'Just plain impossible.' Matt already knew that she didn't like failure. A nimble girl, she was used to succeeding easily at athletic feats.

Master Chang held up one finger. 'Not impossible. When you are ready, bodies and minds will act as one and success will come to you naturally.'

'Oh yeah, and when's that gonna be?' muttered Carl sarcastically. 'Like, some time next century . . .'

'You will be ready when you are ready,' was all Chang would say and, after giving them a few warm-down exercises, he sent them off to get changed.

It was funny, Matt thought, how they'd all arrived at the training session full of pride at yesterday's victory, and now, an hour later, they were all feeling that there was a lot of stuff they still couldn't do. But maybe that was the whole point – winners don't just stay winners, they had to keep pushing themselves . . .

'Hey, Matt – come on!' said Shawn. 'Let's go get breakfast.'

19

Matt hastily finished tying his shoelaces. The session had made him hungry, he realized. He jumped to his feet.

'Race you to the refectory!' he cried.

Chapter 2

MISSING!

The refectory was a spacious, airy hall of modern design, with funky tubular metal chairs and black polished tables you could see your face in. Blown-up photographs of traditional Chinese scenes hung on the walls: pandas, bamboo forests, the Great Wall of China. A long self-service counter offered a fabulous variety of breakfast foods: bacon and eggs and sausages, waffles, fruit, cereal and porridge, as well as the local option of fried noodles. The refectory was noisy and

21

crowded, and they had to wait in line to get to the counter. The delicious smell was making Matt's stomach rumble, and when he reached the front of the queue he piled his plate high.

'Hey – we better be careful we don't get our bellies too full – otherwise the new roll-call machine isn't gonna recognize our silhouettes!' said Catarina.

Everyone laughed. The Academy had installed a new cyber roll-call device on the dorm landing and it was to be activated for the first time that day. It was part of a drive to improve Academy security – and also, Matt thought, because Mr Wu loved the idea of his school being full of the latest hi-tech gadgetry. Mr Wu had been talking proudly about the new system in Assembly the other morning – no other school in the world had anything like it, he'd boasted. The device worked by

recognizing a student's silhouette when
they stepped in front of a ray of fluorescent
light.

From now on, all students would have to be
signed in twice daily – once after lunch and
once in the evening after the school day had
finished. After breakfast, they were all to go
and sign in for the first time, so that the device
could store their silhouettes in its memory.

'It's such a neat idea!' said Shawn. He loved
gadgets of all kinds.

'Yeah,' said Matt. 'It's cool!' It was great to
be part of such a hi-tech Academy; it felt like
living in a school of the future. Then another
thought struck him. 'The only thing is, it may
not be so cool for us. It won't be easy to get
off school premises now.'

'And what would you want to do that for?'
asked Carl.

Carl seemed to have guessed that something

was going on. 'Why would you want to sneak out of school?' he repeated.

Shawn came to the rescue. 'Talking about gadgets, what do you think of this?' He reached into his pocket and took out a shiny silver object, like a large mobile phone, but with a pair of stubby antennae and a display of winking lights. 'My uncle sent it to me.'

'What is it?' asked Catarina.

'Metal detector,' said Shawn. 'See?' He pointed it at Carl's wristwatch – a chunky steel diver's watch – and it began bleeping frantically.

'Well, that's a really useful piece of equipment!' sneered Carl. 'Not! It probably won't work for long anyway, if your dad's alarm system was anything to go by.'

'My dad's alarm system works fine,' said Shawn quietly.

'Come on, you know that system was a

piece of junk – that's how come the thieves broke into the museum –'

'They got in because the system had been turned off!' Shawn said less quietly.

'Yeah, yeah, whatever,' said Carl. 'I bet that metal detector's a piece of junk too!'

'Oh, you do, do you?' said Shawn. 'Watch this – it's got a magnet on it as well!' Still pointing the device at Carl's watch, he raised it and Carl's arm involuntarily shot up in the air. Everyone laughed.

'Hey, quit fooling around!' said Carl angrily.

One of the teachers on duty, Mrs Barraclough, came over to their table. 'Yes, Carl, what is it?'

'Nothing!'

'Oh, I thought you put your hand up.'

Everyone around the table laughed, except for Carl. 'It was just these idiots messing about!' he said.

'I see,' said Mrs Barraclough, moving away.

'I'll get you for that!' said Carl to Shawn.

'Lighten up, Carl!' said Matt. 'It was just a bit of fun.'

'Yeah, well, I didn't find it very funny.' He glared at Shawn, then fell to picking moodily at his food.

The Tangshan Tigers looked at each other and shrugged. Matt speared a sausage and raised it to his mouth. Just as he was about to bite it, the sausage seemed to move away of its own accord.

'What the –' Matt looked in consternation at his fork.

'Don't eat me, don't eat me!' said Shawn, in the kind of high-pitched squeak a sausage might use if it could talk.

'It's you!' said Matt. Shawn was using his gadget to attract the fork. Matt burst out laughing.

'Hey, Shawn – do me!' said Catarina, holding up a fork with noodles wrapped round it. Shawn pointed the gadget again and made the fork move as if to push the noodles into her ear.

Catarina screamed with laughter, and everyone at the table joined in. Except Carl, who pointedly picked up his plate and went to sit at another table. *What could you do with someone like Carl?* Matt wondered. He'd always rather pick a quarrel than take things in a friendly spirit.

After breakfast it was time to go up and have their silhouettes recorded by the cyber roll-call device. It was on the first-floor landing that led to all the dormitories. Matt was impressed by its appearance: it was a milky-white wall panel, with a photo-electric eye mounted on the opposite wall – it looked like some futuristic

device out of a *Star Trek* film. Mr Figgis was
there, marshalling the milling kids into some
sort of order.

'Form a straight line there, please – it only
takes a minute, there's no need to push . . .'

Matt watched as the first student went
and stood in front of the panel – it was an
Indian girl, Shushmita, whom he knew
slightly. Mr Figgis tapped her name into a
keypad beside the electronic eye and pressed
Enter. Immediately there was a blue flash
and Shushmita was illuminated by a ray of
fluorescent light. She gave a nervous giggle.
Her silhouette was picked out, black and
sharp-edged, on the white panel behind her.
After she moved away it remained for a second
or so, before slowly fading away.

'Neat!' said Shawn.

'Next, please!' called Mr Figgis.

The line moved slowly forward. Soon it

was Matt's turn. He stood in place, and gasped
as the fluorescent light suddenly bathed him
– his arms, his legs, his body were a cool
electric blue. When he stepped off the stand
he glanced back and saw, just for an instant, his
own shadow standing there.

Shawn was right. It was neat!

'Hey,' said Matt, after all the sign–ins had been
completed, 'let's go to the Walled Garden. We
need to talk.'

The Walled Garden was a little paved
space behind the common room. It was
secluded, with no windows overlooking it.
There was a cherry tree, its leaves sparse
and yellow at this time of year, and a
wooden bench. It was perfect for private
conversations. Today all squad members
were excused from lessons after their
exertions at the tournament yesterday, but

everyone else would be in class, so they were unlikely to be disturbed.

'What's up?' asked Olivier.

'I was just thinking,' said Matt, 'we should tell Li-Lian about the Jade Dish – how we stopped it being stolen.'

Everyone nodded. 'We couldn't have done it without her,' said Catarina.

'Yeah, we should let her know,' said Shawn.

'Only one problem,' said Olivier. 'This is a city of ten million people. How are we ever going to find her?'

'I know the apartment block she lives in,' said Matt. 'She pointed it out that night she helped us.'

'But do you know the number?' asked Olivier. 'They tend to have kind of large buildings in this city, I've noticed.'

He had a point. The block Li-Lian lived in was enormous – they could hardly go knocking on every single door. Matt frowned, thinking hard. Then his brow cleared.

'I've just remembered something!' he said excitedly. 'You know that market Chang took us to a few weeks ago – there was a girl with a flower-stall there, and I'm sure it was Li-Lian. I thought she looked familiar when we met her!'

The Tigers looked at one another in amazement. But they knew Matt's photographic memory could be trusted.

'Let's get going right away!' said Shawn. 'We don't have any classes today!'

'But we're not supposed to be out without permission,' said Olivier. 'And now they've got that cyber roll-call thing –'

'With a bit of luck, no one will miss us,' said Matt. 'There's a chance we'll get away with it – all the teachers will be in class, won't they? As for the cyber roll-call, we should make it

back just in time for the sign-in if we're quick.
I know it's breaking the rules – but it's for a
good cause. Let's go!'

They went for the front entrance. Sneaking out
of a side-door would make it look as though
they had something to hide. Matt hoped that
if they walked out confidently enough, no one
would challenge them – but as they reached the
atrium, one of the security guards stopped them.

'Where are you going?'

Matt was racking his brains for some excuse,
when to his relief he heard Olivier speak up.

'It's all right, Sam,' he said with a charming
smile. 'We're going out on an errand.'

'You need permission to leave the premises –'

'The martial arts squad have got the day off,'
said Olivier. 'Mr Figgis said we could go to the
museum. Catch you later, Sam.'

He spoke with such confidence that the

guard even touched his peaked cap to them as they passed. The electronic wind-chimes tinkled, and they were outside.

'How did you know his name?' Matt asked as they walked quickly up the road.

'Just through chatting to him. It's a good job it was Sam. The other guy, Eric, is a real stickler. It's always worth getting to know people – you never know when it might come in handy. My dad taught me that!'

Olivier's dad was someone very important in the Swiss diplomatic service.

'But won't we get into trouble?' asked Shawn. 'What if he finds out Mr Figgis didn't give us permission?'

'Why should he speak to Figgis about it? Anyway, it's true – Figgis did say we could go to the museum. Remember the school trip there? It just happened to be a few weeks ago, that's all!'

Matt laughed. It was great the way the Tangshan Tigers all brought different things to the team: Shawn was a techno-wizard, Catarina had breathtaking agility and Olivier's smooth-talking could get them through any situation, however tricky.

'Nice one, Olivier,' he said. 'But listen, we'd better hurry – we've got less than an hour to get there and back!'

They broke into a run.

The market in Jade Moon Street was as crowded as Matt remembered it: lined with stalls, selling everything from caged songbirds to digital cameras, with the market traders calling out their wares at the top of their voices. The road was jammed with people, jostling, stopping to examine the goods on the stalls, haggling with the traders. A Chinese pop song was playing somewhere, and the sweet-spicy scent of fried food, of noodles, dumplings and roast chicken, filled the air.

The Tangshan Tigers pushed through the crowds.

'Are we nearly there, Matt?' asked Catarina urgently. 'We haven't got long!'

'I know – it's just along here, not much further – wait, this looks like it, but –'

There was nobody there. Just an empty barrow with a few scattered petals on it.

'I'm sure this is it,' said Matt, puzzled.

'Let's ask this guy,' said Shawn.

The neighbouring trader ran a fish-stall, piled with multicoloured, glassy-eyed fish, many of which Matt didn't even recognize.

The trader looked up and smiled. He was a small man with a shaved head and a gap in his front teeth that made him look a bit like a pirate. A friendly pirate, though.

'Excuse me,' said Matt, 'we're looking for –'

The man smiled again, and shrugged, and said something in Chinese.

'It's OK,' said Shawn. Mandarin was his father's first language and he spoke it almost as fluently as he spoke English. He chatted to the stall-holder, gesturing at Li-Lian's empty stall. The stall-holder replied at length, pointing down the street.

Shawn turned to the other Tangshan Tigers. 'He says Li-Lian went to pick up an order for some flowers about an hour ago, but that she said she'd only be fifteen minutes. He can't understand what's keeping her.'

'It is a bit strange,' said Matt.

'She might have just stopped off to have tea somewhere,' Catarina suggested.

'She might,' said Matt. 'But I don't think so. Would she leave her stall unattended longer than she needed to? There's something fishy going on – and it's not just that fishmonger's stall!'

'Maybe we should wait?' said Catarina.

'We can wait a bit, but not very —' began
Matt, when Olivier grabbed his arm.

'Look! It's Eric!'

Matt looked. It was the other security guard
from the Academy, the stickler. And he was
making his way through the crowds towards
them.

MYSTERY

'Quick – hide!' said Matt.

They all ducked down behind Li-Lian's empty barrow. Peeping over the top, Matt saw the security guard through the crowds, examining the food on display at a noodle stall.

'He hasn't seen us,' he reported to the others. 'I think he's come here to buy some lunch.'

'Still, maybe we should wait till he's gone?' suggested Shawn.

They waited for a while, but Eric showed no

sign of leaving. He left the first stall and went to another where rabbits and roast chickens were hanging from hooks by their feet.

'We'll miss the sign-in if we don't go soon,' said Matt. 'Quick – while his back's turned. We'll have to run!'

They broke cover and made their way through the packed street as fast as they could. But just as they passed Eric, he turned round and gave a shout. He couldn't have seen their faces, Matt thought, but he must have caught a glimpse of their BIA martial arts outfits.

'Just keep running!' said Matt.

They came out on to the main road. As they were crossing, they glanced back. Olivier groaned. 'He's following us!'

Sure enough, the security guard was on the other side of the road, waiting for a chance to cross. 'Stop!' he shouted.

'Not likely,' muttered Catarina.

'I know a short cut,' said Matt. He had memorized all the streets in the neighbourhood of the Academy. 'If we can get round the next corner before he crosses, we can give him the slip!'

They pelted round the corner, and Matt spied the short cut. He led the Tangshan Tigers down a narrow alley. At once, the noise and bustle of crowds and traffic was left behind.

The alley lay in shadow, with high-walled buildings on either side. They had to skirt past piles of rubbish; at intervals, there were dark, mysterious doorways. As they walked past one of the doorways a rat scuttled out and ran over the toe of Matt's trainer. Matt gasped but there wasn't even time to jump out of the way. The rat had already disappeared through a gap in the wall. Matt couldn't help thinking that this was the type of place you didn't want to spend too long in.

But he didn't feel frightened. Wary, on guard – but not frightened. He used the deep breathing Chang had taught them until he felt his heartbeat slow down. All four of the Tangshan Tigers were walking in step – alert to their surroundings, ready for anything, but cool and confident. Their master's training was working.

Something leapt out of a side turning. A dark blur, a flash of yellow teeth snapped across Matt's line of vision; a ferocious bark echoed off the walls of the alley.

A huge, savage-looking dog had run out of the turning – an ugly beast, its coat the colour of coal, with a massive head and a vicious look in its eyes. It planted itself in their path and barked savagely at them.

Matt faltered – they all did. The Tangshan Tigers looked at each other.

'What should we do?' muttered Shawn.

41

'If we run, it'll be after us in a second,' said Matt.

'Hey, it's only a dog – and we're the Tangshan Tigers, right?' said Catarina. 'We're not going to let a dog make us turn back!'

'We go forward, then,' said Matt. 'Come on!'

They all drew a deep breath. None of the Tigers broke stride as they walked towards the dog.

'No sudden movements,' said Catarina softly. 'And don't stare at it, they hate that. We just walk past, OK?'

They were only a few metres away from the dog; a moment later and they were right on top of it, so close Matt could see the spittle dangling from the animal's jaws. Still they walked firmly, calmly, towards it.

It was a test of nerve, and the dog's nerve broke first. It took a few steps backwards, then sidled against the wall. It stopped barking, and trotted off to sniff at a heap of rubbish, pretending that it hadn't been all that interested in them anyway.

As soon as they got to the end of the alley, they broke into a run again. 'We've only got five minutes!' said Shawn.

They arrived at the Academy, panting for breath, with two minutes to spare. As they ran up the steps, they saw Eric running across the road after them.

'Hey!' he shouted. 'You lot!'

The glass door swished open; the electronic wind-chimes tinkled – and they were inside. The entrance hall was crowded – morning school had just finished and there were lots of kids milling around. Matt and his friends pushed through the other students and dived behind one of the tall white pillars that stood on either side of the school vestibule. In their white martial arts uniforms, they blended in perfectly. Matt poked his head round from behind the pillar. He saw Eric rush in and look wildly around. Then he took off his cap and sat down to get his breath back, scowling.

Matt turned back to his friends. He and the other Tigers grinned at each other.

'Made it!' said Olivier, as they hurried up the stairs to the dorm landing.

'Yeah, but what about Li-Lian?' said Catarina. 'What's happened to her?'

'I dunno,' muttered Matt. 'We need to find out about that – something's not right there.'

'Well, we haven't got time now,' remarked Olivier. 'We've about one minute to get to the presentation!'

They signed their silhouettes in, stepping against the white wall panel until it beeped its approval, and ran down to the Great Hall.

They'd be just in time for the presentation.
None of them wanted to miss that.

Midday. The Great Hall was filling up. Matt
and the Tigers took their places on the stage
with the rest of the team. Carl looked at them
suspiciously.

'Where have you been?' he asked. 'You're all
hot and sweaty. Been for a run?'

'That's right,' said Matt, glancing at his
friends.

The rest of the school was filing in, ready
for the presentation. Everyone seemed excited
at this break in the normal school day – there
was going to be an extended lunch hour
– and there was a pleasant buzz of talking and
laughter.

Mr Wu sat centre-stage, smiling.
Occasionally he reached out to stroke the jade
dish that stood on the table in front of him. He

looked like a contented cat. Beside him was an empty chair, waiting for Chang Sifu.

Matt let his eyes rove over the walls and ceiling of the Great Hall.

It was an impressive space, with a high, vaulted roof, tall windows and a rich and detailed mosaic on the walls, depicting willow trees, lotus flowers and pagodas. The mosaic tiles were heat-sensitive and changed colour throughout the day: early in the morning they were a cool blend of blues, greens and greys, but, as the sun rose in the sky and its rays slanted through the windows, the colours changed. When Matt had first taken his seat the mosaic was a mix of purple, pink and violet, but even in the few minutes they'd waited the colours were lightening and tints of red, yellow and gold began to appear.

Still no appearance from Chang, however. The hall was now full, and the Principal's smile was starting to fade. Matt wondered where Chang could be: he was normally a punctual man and expected his team to be punctual too.

Matt leaned across to Catarina and whispered: 'What's going on?'

Catarina shrugged. 'We wait,' she said, but Matt saw a muscle flicker in her jaw. The other Tangshan Tigers looked at each other in puzzlement. Something wasn't right here: first Li-Lian missing and now Chang. It could be simple coincidence, but two missing people in one day seemed a bit unusual . . .

The other students were getting restless now. There was lots of whispering and shifting around in seats, and shushing from teachers.

Mr Wu leaned towards Miss Lee, his secretary, who was sitting beside him, and whispered furiously in her ear. Miss Lee trotted off the stage and a few moments later an announcement echoed over the public

address system: 'WOULD CHANG SIFU
PLEASE COME TO THE GREAT HALL
IMMEDIATELY?'

Still Chang didn't appear. Now Matt was
sure something was wrong – it was so unlike
Chang to let everyone down. At last, Mr Wu
rose to his feet. He didn't look happy.

'Unfortunately we cannot make the
presentation today, since Chang Sifu is not
present. We cannot have a ceremony without
the man who led our team to victory. I can
only assume he is indisposed. School dismissed.
There will be no extended lunch hour today.'

There was a collective groan, and then the
school started to file out again.

The squad were left sitting on the stage,
unsure what to do.

'It's no use sitting there,' said Mr Wu sharply.
'Go to your rooms. Or to the library to work.
Disperse!'

He went down the steps and clicked briskly out of the hall.

Matt and the Tigers gathered outside.

'What shall we do?' said Matt.

'Maybe we should go to his room and see – maybe he's ill or something . . .?' said Shawn.

'Come on, then!' said Matt.

Chang Sifu's office was at the end of a long corridor. As they approached, they saw Chang's door open and Mr Wu stormed out, his face like thunder.

'It is no use looking here,' he snapped. 'Your teacher is not in his office.' He pushed past them and was gone.

'Chang might not be there,' said Matt. 'But there might be some clue. Let's go in.'

Chang's name was written on the door in both Chinese characters and the Roman alphabet. Matt pushed the door open.

Chang's office was neat and austere.

And empty. A desk and chair, a computer, some Chinese books on a shelf. The only decoration was a painting on the wall. Matt went over to look at it more closely. It depicted a tiger pacing down the length of the scroll. A range of mountains rose in the background. It was painted in a graceful Chinese style, with neat, economical strokes of the brush.

'The tiger,' said Shawn. 'It's a symbol of Chinese strength and beauty.'

'Hey, look!' said Catarina. She pointed to a bouquet of flowers lying on the desk.

'Like the ones Li-Lian sells,' said Matt. 'Do you think it's a clue?'

'There's a note wrapped round it!' said Olivier. He snatched up the piece of paper, frowned, then handed it to Shawn.

Shawn translated aloud. 'We have someone you value very much. You want her back unharmed. You know what we need.'

There was a short silence.

Matt grabbed the note. He held it up to the light, looking for a clue, a watermark or hidden message, but there was nothing – just rows of neat Chinese characters.

'Who's it from?' asked Catarina.

'It's not signed,' said Shawn.

'Sounds like a ransom note!' said Olivier.

'Yeah,' said Catarina. 'But who's been kidnapped?'

'It's got to be Li-Lian!' said Matt. 'We know she's gone missing – and the flowers prove it! Remember she said her grandfather was a great man? She must have meant Chang!'

'And that's where Chang's gone,' said Shawn. 'He's gone to find her!'

'But it doesn't make sense!' said Catarina. 'Chang's not a rich man – I mean, he gets a teacher's salary, but that's all. Why kidnap his granddaughter?'

'And you don't get rich doing martial arts,' said Shawn. 'Not unless you do movies –'

'Hold on, hold on,' said Matt. 'We don't know what the kidnappers want from him, but that's not the point. The point is, Chang must have gone off to try and rescue Li-Lian – why else would he disappear? And we've got to help him.'

'Right!' said Shawn. 'I mean, he's done so much for us.'

'This is our chance to do something for him!' said Olivier.

'Yeah!' said Matt. 'This is a job for the Tangshan Tigers!'

'Sure,' said Catarina. 'But how are we going to find him? China's, like, a big country, you know?'

'I think I know how we might track him down,' said Olivier. 'Take a look at this.' His sharp eyes had spotted a book lying open on top of a shelf. He picked it up and laid it on the desk. 'It's an atlas of China – and a page has been ripped out!'

'I bet that's where he's gone!' said Shawn. 'Wherever the missing page showed, that's where Chang is headed right now.'

'Looks like it,' said Catarina. 'But it's not much use to us if he took the page with him!'

'Hey, but I bet there's another copy in the school library,' said Matt. 'Let's go!'

SEARCHING FOR SIFU

The library was a state-of-the-art building on several floors with high smoked-glass windows and a deep-pile carpet that muffled the sound of footsteps. Every desk had a computer terminal, and it didn't take Shawn long to find the atlas in the electronic catalogue.

'Here it is!'

'Great!' said Matt. 'What shelf number is it?'

'No need to bother with that!' said Shawn. 'I can find it online – look.'

He stabbed at the keyboard and the page,

the one that had been missing from Chang Sifu's copy, filled the screen. Matt and the others clustered around, peering over Shawn's shoulder.

The page showed a built-up area to the north of Beijing. 'At least he hasn't gone far!' said Matt.

'But how're we gonna find him?' demanded Catarina. 'These streets, there's hundreds all over the page, like spaghetti!'

'Look!' said Olivier. 'There's Changping train station – I'd guess that's where he's headed. It serves the whole north of the country. That would explain why he left so suddenly – he had a train to catch!'

'Yes – I bet you're right!' said Matt. 'Anyhow, that's our best guess. Let's go!'

'Let's go where?' asked Shawn. 'To Changping station?'

'Sure,' said Matt. 'Where else?'

'But we've got to sign in for the roll-call later, and Changping's quite a way – what if we don't get back?'

Matt smiled and put his hand on Shawn's shoulder. 'Well, that's where you come in, Shawn. I bet there isn't a gadget on earth you can't take apart and put back together and make it do exactly what you want! Couldn't you sort out that cyber roll-call machine?'

Shawn smiled. 'Well, I guess . . . Now you mention it . . .'

It was quiet on the first-floor landing. Nearly all the school were back in class – except for the other squad members, most of whom were resting in their rooms.

Everyone watched, fascinated, as Shawn got to work with a tiny screwdriver he kept on his key-ring. Beside the photo-electric eye was a black metal panel, which Shawn deftly unscrewed and removed. A small screen was revealed, with a row of different-coloured buttons beneath it.

'Looks complicated,' said Matt.

Shawn snorted. 'It's totally simple! Watch.'

He pressed one of the buttons and a list of names came up on-screen. 'That's the memory, right? I could just delete all our names and we'd be fine. But then we'd have the hassle of reprogramming it with our silhouettes again later. So I'm going to do something a little bit smarter.'

Using the touchpad, he highlighted the names of the Tangshan Tigers one by one; then he pressed another button and the window named Settings appeared on-screen. 'I'm just altering the settings to skip our four names when it comes to the sign-in,' Shawn explained, as his fingers flickered over the buttons with bewildering speed. 'Now the machine thinks we're permanently signed in!'

'So we can come and go as we please!' said Olivier.

'Yeah, and we'd better go!' said Matt. 'If Chang's catching a train, we haven't got much time to lose!'

'We have to get our coats,' said Olivier.

'And we'd better get some stuff together,' said Catarina. 'We'll need food, water –'

'And I've got a compass in my room,' said Shawn. 'May come in useful.'

'OK, but hurry,' said Matt. 'Meet you in the foyer in five minutes!'

Five and a half minutes later and they were outside, running down the street.

It was a bright day in late autumn, with a pale sun glaring from a clear sky. Despite the seriousness of the situation, Matt felt fantastic to be out in the open, setting off on an adventure. The Tangshan Tigers were on the trail again!

'We should cross here,' panted Shawn, consulting his compass as he ran. 'North's that way.'

'I know,' said Matt. His photographic memory had automatically recorded the route from the map. 'We go up that road, then left, then second right.'

Soon they had left the skyscrapers of Beijing behind. They crossed another main road. They were entering a more residential district, with smaller houses and low-rise apartment blocks with washing-lines strung out on the balconies. The streets were less crowded here. But soon they entered a commercial quarter, with shops and offices, and buses trundling along the main roads. Half-finished houses were surrounded with bamboo scaffolding.

It was a side of Beijing Matt had never seen before.

As they ran, Matt anxiously scanned the streets, searching for a glimpse of their master. Suddenly, his heart gave a leap. Through the crowds of pedestrians he'd caught a glimpse of a familiar figure – it was Chang, wearing the kingfisher-blue silk jacket he favoured when he was not in his combat attire. He was striding purposefully along.

'There he is!' shouted Matt.

'I saw him too!' said Olivier.

'Where?' said Catarina.

'Come on!' said Matt.

They increased their pace, dodging round passers-by. Shawn stumbled; they stopped to help him up. It was only a moment's delay, but when Matt looked again Chang's blue silk jacket had disappeared – all Matt could see was hundreds of people milling about.

'Master Chang!' shouted Matt at the top of his voice. People nearby turned to stare. Chang seemed to have vanished into thin air.

They stopped at an intersection, getting their breath back while they waited for a chance to cross.

'I know that was Chang!' said Matt. 'Where could he have got to?'

'Wherever he went, we lost him,' said Catarina.

'We'd better carry on to the station!' said Olivier. 'Maybe we can still find him there.'

A gentle cough sounded just above their heads. 'Perhaps I can save you trouble,' said a familiar voice. 'There is no need to proceed to station.'

Matt looked up and saw Chang sitting cross-legged halfway up the bamboo scaffolding on a building under construction. Matt felt a wave of relief surge through him.

'Master Chang!' shouted the Tangshan Tigers, more or less in unison.

With an easy, athletic grace, Chang swung down from the scaffolding and landed on the pavement beside them.

'You knew we were following you!' said Matt.

'Oh yes. You took little pains to conceal yourselves. It was less like being pursued by Tangshan Tigers than pursued by Tangshan Elephants!' Chang Sifu gave one of his rare smiles.

Matt drew in his breath sharply. He and the other Tigers looked at each other in amazement. So Chang knew about the Tangshan Tigers?

'But, how did you –' Matt began.

Chang held up one finger. 'I know many things. But, now, a question for you. How did you find me?'

'We saw the flowers and the note in your study,' explained Shawn. 'And the map with the page torn out –'

'So we came to see what we could do to help!' continued Matt. He waited for Chang to look pleased by the offer of help. But Chang's smile had already faded away and his face was serious.

'I thank you for your loyalty – and your courage,' he said gravely. 'But you must return to the Academy now. You have no idea – none – what is at stake.'

'But we're the Tangshan Tigers!' said Catarina. 'We can handle it, whatever it is!'

'The Tangshan Tigers is a wonderful idea. But you are not ready for situation like this. Truly, you must let me handle alone.' He looked past them into the distance. 'These are dangerous people,' he said quietly.

Matt took a step towards him, his hands held

open. He had to persuade Chang to let them help him. Chang had done so much for them; they couldn't lose this chance to do something in return.

'Master Chang,' he said, 'the strong man accepts help; the weak man struggles on alone.'

Matt knew that quoting Chang's own words back at him might sound impertinent; but he didn't mean it that way. He hoped Chang would understand.

Master Chang looked at him for a long, slow moment, his face expressionless. 'I am touched that you wish to help. But you should be in school. It is my duty to send you back there.'

'But we've got the day off to recuperate!' said Catarina. 'After the tournament.'

'This is not exactly recuperation,' said Chang.

Matt didn't dare say anything. No one else spoke either.

Chang looked at them all in turn and seemed to come to a decision.

Then he gave a single nod.

'Train leaves in fifteen minutes,' he said. 'I must explain as we walk. There is no time to lose.' He turned and started walking, so fast that the Tigers had to trot to keep up. 'My granddaughter has been kidnapped.'

'Is that – Li-Lian?' said Matt.

Chang's stride slowed down for a moment. He smiled and nodded to himself – as if something had just been confirmed to him.

'She helped us out when we were, er, visiting the museum.'

'Ah,' said Chang. 'Li-Lian told me she had helped a group of Western children. So it was the Tangshan Tigers . . .'

The station was in view now, at the end of the

65

road – a wide-fronted grey building with the red, gold-starred Chinese flag flying over it, and rows of taxis parked outside. Chang quickened his pace.

'We have just time to buy tickets,' he said. 'We are going to Miyun.'

'Where's that?' asked Shawn.

'You will see. If we do not miss the train!'

The train rolled out of the station, slowly at first, but quickly picking up speed. Matt saw concrete office and apartment blocks through the window, then a more industrial landscape of factories and warehouses, then a few green spaces began to appear. They were leaving the city behind.

They had the carriage almost to themselves: there was an elderly couple chatting quietly in Mandarin at one end, and a family who were noisily cracking and eating nuts at the other end, and in between a young woman in glasses, who looked like a student, reading a book. Apart from that, there was nobody but Chang and the Tangshan Tigers.

Chang distributed the food he'd bought at a station kiosk for the journey – some prawn and vegetable dumplings, some fruit, a bottle of water each.

'So, what's at Miyun?' asked Olivier, as they ate.

'A bamboo forest,' said Chang. 'And a reservoir.'

'Which one are we going to?'

'Bamboo forest.'

'Is that where the kidnappers are?'

Chang shook his head. 'Many, many years ago, I was entrusted with a key. A key of gold. My task – to keep it safe. It is this key that the kidnappers want. Not for itself, but for what it unlocks. What it unlocks is beyond price.'

67

'And what's that?' asked Matt breathlessly.

'No need for details. Enough to say, kidnappers will shrink from nothing to get this key. Which I no longer have.'

There was a general gasp. 'What?' said Matt. 'But it's not lost, is it? A key so valuable, I can't believe –' He stopped, not wanting to sound as though he was accusing Master Chang of being careless.

'You are right not to believe it,' said Chang mildly. 'I did not lose it, but put in safe place. Very safe place. I put in bamboo forest.'

'In a forest?' said Catarina. 'But anything could have happened – someone could have picked it up, or a – a magpie could have stolen it, or –'

'I made small slit in stalk of young bamboo tree,' Chang explained. 'And I pushed key into it. That bamboo shoot will be a fully grown tree by now. As I said, it is a very, very safe place.'

'But how did you expect you'd ever find it again?' said the outspoken Catarina.

'I hoped I would never have to find it. That key unlocks things that were better left locked. Now, I have no choice. I must go back to the forest and find the key.'

'But how?' asked Olivier.

Chang Sifu folded his hands in his lap. 'I will find it,' he said heavily. He closed his eyes. He did not say any more.

The Tangshan Tigers exchanged glances. No one dared say anything, but Matt knew they were all thinking the same thing. What were the chances of finding the key after all these years?

An hour later, the train pulled into Miyun. No one spoke much as they disembarked from the train and left the station.

'This way,' said Chang.

The Tangshan Tigers followed him along a quiet road with little traffic; as they rounded a bend, Miyun Forest came into view, an ocean of green extending as far as the eye could see. It was, thought Matt, a completely different world, almost a different planet from the crowded, hectic city of Beijing.

'Down here,' said Chang.

He led them down a rutted track, and presently they were standing at the edge of the forest. The pale brown bamboo stems soared about fifteen metres into the air; the green leaves swayed and bobbed in the afternoon breeze. Somewhere, they could hear the distant chirping of a bird. You could hardly see any distance into the forest, the bamboo stems were so close together and the shadows so dark.

Talk about a needle in a haystack, thought Matt. Finding a needle in a haystack would be easy compared with this. If you sifted through all the hay, you'd come upon the needle eventually. But a golden key in a bamboo forest?

THE BAMBOO FOREST

'Well, hey,' said Catarina, 'might as well get on with it!'

She launched a flying kick at the nearest bamboo tree.

The stem shivered and shook, but did not break. She attacked it with her hands, delivering a rapid volley of karate chops.

'Wait,' said Chang quietly. 'This is not the way. You must not attack the trees. We must use our heads.'

'But what are we going to do?' asked Matt.

'If we don't chop the bamboo down, how can we see what's inside it?'

'We gotta use force,' said Catarina. 'We can't meditate our way to the key!'

Chang gave one of his faint half-smiles. 'Meditation can achieve much. But for this task, I think I would prefer to use fancy metal detector of Shawn's.'

'How did you . . .?' Shawn began. His voice tailed away. Matt grinned. Of course, Chang knew everything. Or at least everything he needed to know.

'But before we use metal detector, we should take care of one who follows us.'

The Tangshan Tigers stared at Chang, then at each other.

'What?' said Shawn and Catarina in unison, while Olivier said, 'Excuse me?'

Chang put a finger to his lips. He stepped into the shade of the bamboo trees and beckoned to the Tangshan Tigers. They went a little way into the forest until they were hidden from view, and Chang motioned for them to stop. He pointed back at the clearing.

Through the bamboo stems, Matt saw a figure run into the clearing. He had to stop himself exclaiming aloud in surprise. It was Carl Warrick. What on earth was Carl doing here?

Carl looked around on all sides. He exclaimed loudly when he saw he was alone. He glared at the forest, but Matt and his friends were invisible in the shadows. Matt could see him thinking, as clearly as if he'd spoken aloud: *They must be in that forest, and how am I ever gonna find them in there?*

He turned away and launched a few frustrated karate kicks into thin air, shouting. Matt grinned, and saw that Catarina, Shawn and Olivier were smiling too. It was hard not to laugh at the sight of Carl, venting all his anger by kicking a non-existent opponent.

Chang silently moved forward to the edge of the clearing. Matt and the others followed as quietly as they could.

'Hello, Carl,' said Chang softly but very distinctly.

Startled, Carl froze in mid-kick. He stood on one leg like a stork for a second, then teetered and fell on his back.

He scrambled to his feet as Chang and the Tangshan Tigers came out to meet him. He brushed the dust off himself and faced them with a mixture of embarrassment and defiance.

'What are you doing here, Carl?' asked Chang.

'I followed these guys when I saw them leave the school. Is there a problem with that? I mean, if they can do it, why can't I?'

He had a point there, Matt had to admit.

'But why did you follow us?' asked Catarina.

'I–I just wanted to find out what you guys were up to. You're always sloping off together – I was just . . . curious, OK? No law against that, is there?'

Chang folded his arms and gazed at Carl, as if the answer to what he should do with him could be read in his face. After a few moments Chang gave an almost imperceptible nod.

'Well, you are here now,' he said, not unkindly. 'I am responsible for your safety and cannot send you back to Academy alone. It is best you come with us.'

The Tangshan Tigers looked at each other in disappointment.

'Cool!' said Carl. 'Where are we going?'

'Into the forest,' said Chang.

Once again, they stepped into the shadowy world of the bamboo forest. 'Tread with care,' said Chang softly. 'Do not drop anything or damage surroundings. This is a special place.'

'Yeah, right, just a load of old trees –' began Carl, but stopped as the Tangshan Tigers glared at him.

The forest was beautiful. The little light that filtered through the trees had a greeny–gold glow to it, and the air smelt rich and earthy. The trees grew close together and soared straight up, far straighter than the gnarled trees of an English forest, to a leafy canopy high above their heads.

'Hold metal detector straight out, Shawn,' said Chang. 'We are somewhere near, I think.'

He was scanning the trees closely as he spoke. Suddenly, he gave a low exclamation. The others followed the direction of his eyes. Matt saw one of the bamboo stems quiver. As Shawn got nearer, it swayed and began to lean towards him like a live thing.

'You may switch off, Shawn,' said Chang. 'We do not wish to damage tree.'

He felt carefully over the bark and his hands settled on a raised scar. His strong fingers prised it apart. With a little exclamation of triumph, he drew out a small golden key with an iron chain, and displayed it in the palm of his hand. The key glinted dully in the green half-light.

'Sweet!' said Matt. 'Mission accomplished!'

'Not quite yet,' said Chang. 'We have a long journey to make.'

'Where are we going?' asked Matt.

'We are going,' said Chang, 'to the Great Wall of China, at Huanghua.'

'Oh wow!' said Matt. His heart gave a bound of excitement. They were going to see one of the wonders of the world. He had seen pictures of the Great Wall, of course, and Mr Figgis had taught them about it in history –

but to see it first-hand, up close, that would be something else. Glancing around he saw that the other Tigers shared his excitement. Shawn's eyes were bright. Even Carl looked interested.

'But the way is long,' said Chang. 'We must rest here tonight, at the edge of the forest.'

'Won't we get into trouble when we go back to the Academy, though?' asked Matt. 'They're bound to spot it if we stay away a whole night!'

'You have an English saying, I think: "We will cross that bridge when we come to it."' said Chang.

They found a small, sandy clearing, and Chang quickly built a fire-pit of stones. They all collected dry wood, and Chang lit the fire with a box of matches he produced from the leather shoulder-bag he had brought with him. He also produced what was left of the food he had bought at the station. There wasn't a great deal to go round, but just enough to keep them from going hungry.

'Oh, man, this is so delicious!' said Catarina.

'It's fantastic!' said Matt. 'Thanks, Master Chang!' He was starving, and the food was just what he needed – and eating it at the edge of the great forest, sitting around a crackling campfire, made it taste even better.

'It's the best meal I've ever tasted!' said Shawn.

'You can't have tasted many good meals then!' said Carl. 'I remember going to this restaurant in Sydney one time, and –'

'Oh, yeah,' said Olivier, in a perfect imitation of Carl's Australian accent, 'and we had barbecued shark stuffed with jellyfish! That was something else!'

Everyone laughed. Even Chang smiled faintly. Carl scowled, and finished his food in silence.

It was getting dark now. The stars were coming out, bright and twinkling in the clear navy-blue sky. Matt noticed how close Carl sat to the fire, staring at the flames as if they protected him from the gathering darkness. Carl looked tired. He couldn't stop yawning, and presently he lay down, mumbling that he was just going to have a little rest. Almost immediately he was fast asleep.

Chang carefully laid a coat over him. Then he beckoned to the Tangshan Tigers, and led them a small distance away from the fire.

'It is good that Carl sleeps,' he said. 'The time has come to share with you the secret of the golden key.'

THE SECRETS OF THE KEY

The sky was a velvet black now, except for the twinkling silver dots of the stars and a thin crescent moon. The dying campfire gave off a reddish-orange glow. There was no sound but the chirping of crickets as Chang began his story.

'I did not explain before. I did not know whether I would find key, and to tell whole story might not have been necessary. Now we have the key and you are coming with me on journey, it is best you know something of what this is all about.

'Know, then, that this golden key is one
of seven. Each of the seven keys is held by a
respected, esteemed household in different
provinces of China. Twenty years ago, these
keys were given to us by our superiors
– powerful men, with best interests of
China at heart, but ageing, who trusted us
to protect secret after their death. So each
keyholder is – or was – a person who
could be trusted absolutely. The seven keys
together unlock cavern of untold wealth. I do
not exaggerate – measureless, inexhaustible
wealth. All seven keyholders swore we
would not use keys. We would leave riches
undisturbed.'

Matt listened intently, totally absorbed
in Chang's story. It was fascinating to hear
about these important, secret events that had
occurred years before he was born.

'So it was for twenty years,' went on Chang.

'But now, times change. Two of the first keyholders have died, and their sons do not wish to keep the vows their fathers made. The others have fallen on hard times, or are greedy for profit.

'And so the six keyholders have united and asked me to surrender seventh key – in return for a seventh share of the wealth, be it understood. I replied that I made a vow and reasons for keeping it are as strong now as they were then. I would not give up the key.

'Result: these people became desperate. They kidnapped Li-Lian. And now I have no choice but to hand over key.'

'What if you don't?' asked Catarina.

'They will kill her,' said Chang. 'There is not slightest doubt of that. So, you see, I have no choice.'

There was a pause.

Matt felt disturbed by Chang's story. He remembered their meeting with Li-Lian outside the museum, and how delicate she'd looked in the moonlight, how friendly and trusting she had been.

'I know an honourable soul when I see one,' she'd said. Now she was being held prisoner by men who were far from honourable. It was horrible to think of gentle Li-Lian in the hands of such ruthless people.

At the same time, Matt was puzzled by Chang's explanation. It did not seem quite complete.

'What is this untold wealth?' he asked. 'And why can't it be touched?'

Chang shook his head. 'I cannot give more details. It is very dangerous secret, better that you do not know, unless it becomes absolutely necessary. It is enough that you know I must hand over key. Otherwise . . .'

A look of pain crossed his normally calm features. Matt felt a stab of sympathy.

'Anything we can do . . .' he said.

'Thank you,' said Chang gravely. 'I may say it is some comfort, simply you being here. But I am reluctant to take you down the dangerous path that lies ahead.'

Matt thrust out his fist, palm down. Olivier brought his hand down on top of Matt's fist. Catarina put her hand on top of Olivier's and Shawn placed his hand on top of hers. All four of them glanced up at Chang Sifu. He lifted a hand and let it rest in the air above theirs. Then he brought his open palm down on the back of Shawn's hand.

'Thank you,' he said quietly. 'This means a lot to me.' The vow had been made without any need for words. They would help their master rescue Li-Lian.

And, Matt thought but did not say aloud, *if*

we can find a way to rescue her without giving up the key, we will!

Matt was woken early next morning by the call of a bird – thin and clear in the chilly air. His limbs felt stiff, and he was cold. Chang was already awake, feeding sticks into the fire, which he had re-animated. The Tangshan Tigers stirred, yawning and stretching. Carl was the last to wake. He pulled himself into a sitting position and complained: 'I'm freezing. And I ache all over. I couldn't sleep at all, that was the worst night's sleep I've ever had!'

Which was strange, thought Matt, because Carl had snored heartily all through the night.

'When you are up and walking, coldness and stiffness will pass,' Chang told him. 'And we must hurry. We have train to Huanghua to catch, and missing it would be disaster.'

'What's for breakfast?' asked Carl grumpily.

'No breakfast,' said Chang. 'Just this.' He held out five peeled twigs.

'We've got to eat sticks?' said Carl incredulously. 'What are we, pandas?'

'Not to eat,' said Chang patiently. 'To clean teeth. Rub teeth and gums gently, then rinse.' He held out a canister of water. 'Fresh from spring.'

Matt cleaned his teeth, rinsed and spat, then drank some of the cool, fresh-tasting water.

Five minutes later they were on their way back to the station, trotting to keep up with the brisk pace set by Chang.

At the station, things weren't good. It was pandemonium. Crowds were seething around, people were shouting, a loudspeaker blared out incomprehensible announcements and there were uniformed police everywhere.

'What's happening?' asked Matt.

'Police are carrying out security check,' said Chang shortly. He pointed to a sleek red train on the other side of a metal barrier. 'That is Huanghua train. It leaves in ten minutes. We must get through.'

He stopped a policeman and spoke to him urgently in Mandarin. The policeman answered curtly and pointed to a line of people queuing up for a checkpoint at the barrier. For the first time ever, Matt saw the colour drain from Chang's cheeks.

'What'd he say?' asked Matt.

'We've got to queue up to have the bag checked,' Shawn translated. 'There's been a security alert and they're not letting anyone through until their luggage has been checked. He says if we miss the train it's just bad luck.'

'But it's more than bad luck!' said Matt. 'If we don't get to the Great Wall at the time they said –'

'Can't we jump the barrier?' suggested Catarina.

'Not wise,' said Chang, who had finished his conversation with the policeman and now shepherded them to join the queue. 'These officers are armed and will shoot.'

Matt felt anxiety crawl through him as the line moved slowly forward. 'What if we miss the train?' he muttered.

'If we miss it we must make another plan, and swiftly,' said Chang. He had recovered his composure and was his usual calm self again. 'But let us hope we do not miss it.'

The police were searching the bags thoroughly but briskly, and though the queue seemed to move with agonizing slowness, they were getting closer to the front. They reached the head of the line with three minutes to spare.

The officer at the checkpoint was a cold–

eyed man with a neat black beard. He roughly ordered Chang to open his leather case. Chang opened it; the man snatched it from him and emptied it on to the table. A few modest possessions tumbled out – the box of matches, a razor, a small towel and so on – and lastly the gold key, which clattered across the wooden surface.

The policeman picked it up and examined it closely, turning it this way and that. He rapped out a question in Mandarin, which Matt didn't understand but which obviously meant, 'What's this?'

Chang replied in polite, respectful tones, with much bowing of the head. Matt felt sweat spring out on the palms of his hands. They now had less than two minutes to spare by the big station clock overhead. What if the policeman wouldn't let them through? What if he confiscated the key? He hoped that Carl, with his usual knack of blurting out the wrong thing at the wrong time, wouldn't say anything to annoy the officer. But when he looked, he saw that Carl, not having any luggage to be searched, had already slipped through and was on the other side of the barrier, swaggering cockily around, pleased with himself at being the first one through.

The police officer swept everything back into the bag, including the key, and threw it on top of a pile of luggage on a table behind him. He said something to Chang – Shawn hastily whispered a translation for the others. 'They're keeping it for further inspection. We can wait till later, or board the train without it!'

Chang bowed his head, and, without a word, passed through the barrier. Silently, Matt and the others followed.

Once they'd gone a little way down the platform, Chang stopped. The Tangshan Tigers

clustered around him in dismay. Carl was
further down the platform, out of earshot,
scaring pigeons. The train left in one minute
– but what was the point in getting on it
without the key?

'What are we going to do, sir?' asked Matt.

'If we haven't got the key –' said Olivier.

'How can we save Li-Lian?' said Shawn.

'All that effort getting it –'

'And they just take it off us –'

'It's a disaster!' said Olivier.

Chang held up his hand for silence. He
looked at the station clock. He looked back
at the pile of luggage. Then he looked at
Catarina.

'Is your agility ready to be tested?' he asked.

Catarina grinned. 'Sure thing!'

'Meet us on the train, then,' said Chang.
'Matt, Shawn, Olivier, come with me.'

He led them down the platform, following

Carl who had gone on ahead. Matt glanced behind him and saw Catarina running back towards the checkpoint.

Chang opened the door of one of the carriages and motioned them on board. Just as Matt was getting on, he saw Catarina leap on to a station wagon and launch herself from there up into the wooden rafters of the roof. She looked down, caught Matt's eye and winked.

They took their seats on the train. Carl, who hadn't noticed Catarina at all, announced that he was going to find the buffet car and get himself some breakfast.

Through the window, Matt saw Catarina swinging herself from rafter to rafter with amazing agility. The other Tigers piled to the window next to Matt, craning their necks to watch.

'Oh, man!' said Shawn. 'She's so cool – like a circus acrobat!'

Catarina was now only a little behind the checkpoint officer, about two metres above his head. The officer remained oblivious as Catarina hooked her legs over the rafter and let herself dangle upside down.

'I don't believe it!' said Olivier. 'How long can she hang on like that?'

Matt glanced round at Chang Sifu, to see what he thought of it. But Chang wasn't even looking – he had taken a book from his pocket and was calmly reading.

Catarina was directly above the pile of luggage. The other police officers on duty were too busy to think of looking up into the rafters. The only people who did see Catarina were those waiting in the queue for that checkpoint – Matt noticed the woman at the front give a faint start of surprise, then smile and look away. No one in the line said a word. Matt guessed the police had been so heavy-handed in carrying out their duties that no one wanted to help them.

Catarina's long slender arms reached down towards the pile of confiscated luggage. Matt held his breath. Could she get away with it?

Fortunately, Chang's case was at the top, just within reach. Her knuckles grazed the handle, but couldn't quite grasp it.

'Oh no!' gasped Olivier. 'She's missed it!'

Catarina let herself dangle a little lower. The strain on her leg muscles must have been immense – could she hold on?

She gave an extra stretch, as if she had somehow found another centimetre of arm, and her fingers closed round the handle of Chang's bag.

'Yes!' shouted Matt. 'She's done it!'

Catarina swung back up into the rafters, and started swinging her way back towards the platform.

But now, Matt realized with a shock, the train was moving. It had started so smoothly he hadn't noticed, but the station wall was gliding by outside the window. And it was picking up speed every second.

Catarina hit the ground running. She was chasing after the train for all she was worth, her long legs flying over the ground. Matt wanted to open the window and shout, 'Come on, Catarina, you can do it!' But he knew he mustn't draw attention to her, or she'd be caught. All he could do was watch helplessly. The train was accelerating all the time. She wasn't getting any nearer.

The train track curved, and as the train went round the bend, Matt lost sight of Catarina. Then everything went black. They had entered a tunnel.

Just then, Carl reappeared with a can of coke and packet of crisps. 'Breakfast time!'

he said. No one took any notice of him.

Matt felt sick with disappointment. Catarina had got so close! If the train had been delayed a mere ten seconds she would have been fine. As it was, she was stuck on the platform with the golden key and they were speeding away from her. Matt looked at Master Chang. To his surprise, Chang looked as calm as usual – even quietly pleased.

'Hi, guys!'

Matt spun round in his seat. There was Catarina, striding down the carriage towards them, jauntily swinging Chang's leather bag.

'But you . . .' said Matt, his voice trailing off. 'There's no way you could have caught the train.'

Catarina smiled as she sat down with them. 'You should have more faith in me.'

'Yay!' shouted Shawn. 'Way to go, Catarina!'

The Tangshan Tigers cheered and clapped.

Carl had no idea what all the fuss was about, and just shrugged.

'Thank you, Catarina,' said Chang as he reached out for the bag. He spoke matter-of-factly, as though Catarina had just brought him a sandwich from the buffet car.

Catarina threw herself into a seat, blew away a strand of dark hair that had fallen over her face and grinned triumphantly.

'That was sweet, Catarina,' said Matt, punching her shoulder.

They settled down for the journey.

Next stop, Huanghua and the Great Wall of China.

And a meeting with the kidnappers.

THE GREAT WALL

'Oh, wow!' said Matt. He was standing on the Great Wall of China. Actually standing on it.

It was high, reaching up some six metres from the ground. Matt shaded his eyes from the sun and gazed at the view of fields, hills and a glittering blue reservoir. It was wider than he'd imagined – easily wide enough to drive a car down. But there were no cars, of course, only tourists on foot, exclaiming at the views and taking photographs.

The Wall was built of massive blocks of

weathered grey stone, some of them crumbly. It sprouted tall stone towers at regular intervals, dwindling in apparent size as the wall snaked away to the horizon.

'It's fantastic!' said Matt. 'How far does it go on for?'

'It is known as *wan li chang cheng*,' said Chang. 'This translates as wall of ten thousand li – or five thousand kilometres, in other words.'

'And how old is it?'

'It was built over many centuries. The very oldest sections are over two thousand years old.'

'Yeah, it looks like it!' said Carl. 'It's falling to pieces!' He sprang up on to the parapet and kicked at one of the crumbling stones. A shower of fragments and dust fell to the ground.

'Carl!' said Chang sharply. 'Get down

immediately! You will please to respect this ancient monument.'

It was unusual for Chang to raise his voice, and the effect on Carl was immediate. He sheepishly descended from the parapet.

'So – where do we go from here?' asked Olivier.

'This way,' said Chang. He led them along the wall. This section was flat and easy to walk along. It was quite crowded, so that they had to weave their way through slow-moving parties of tourists.

After a few hundred metres, however, it rose up very steeply, and most of the tourists turned back at this point. Soon, they had left the crowds behind completely. The noise of their chatter died away, and there was no sound but the sighing of the wind.

They came to an opening in the side of the wall. Without a word, Chang led them through it and down a flight of steps, which took them to the base of the wall.

Matt saw Chang stroking a hand along the rough stone, carefully, attentively, as if feeling for something, probing the cracks between the stones. After a while he settled on one particular block. He gave four sharp raps, one at each corner.

Matt gasped. A black opening in the wall was appearing, as a section slid smoothly, noiselessly to one side. It was like magic.

An opening the size of a doorway was revealed.

'That's amazing!' said Shawn.

'Yeah, it's pretty neat,' Carl conceded, as though he was some sort of expert judge of sliding wall sections. 'Not bad. So now what happens?'

Chang stepped to one side and motioned for them to enter. The Tangshan Tigers stepped in. It was very dark, and very cool – like being inside a cave. The autumn sunshine, though they could still see it through the opening, seemed to belong to another world.

'I'm standing inside the Great Wall of China,' Matt said to himself. The thought was astounding, unbelievable. And all those tourists milling around up on top of the wall – not one of them had an inkling that this secret chamber existed under their feet.

Carl was still outside, peering in. 'Could one of you guys turn the light on?'

'There is no light, Carl,' said Chang. 'Please to enter; we are waiting for you.'

'No way!' said Carl. 'I'm not going in there without the light on – haven't they heard of electricity around here?'

There was a hint of nervousness in his voice. And suddenly Matt got it. Carl was afraid of the dark! Swaggering, cocksure Carl was afraid

of the dark. For an instant Matt was tempted
to burst out laughing. But he checked himself.
It would be cruel – Carl looked miserable
enough already. And making him angry was
only likely to lead to trouble.

'You do not wish to enter, Carl?' said Chang,
his voice gentler now. 'Very well. No one will
make you do anything you do not wish to do.
You can wait for us here.'

'Suits me fine,' shrugged Carl. 'But how long
are you guys gonna be?'

'That is hard to tell,' replied Chang. 'Difficult
to judge.'

He stepped into the chamber with the
Tangshan Tigers.

'Do you think he'll be OK out there on his
own?' asked Olivier.

'He should not come to harm,' said Chang
quietly. 'He will probably be safer there than if
he came with us.'

He rapped on another part of the wall
and the missing section slid back into place,
blotting out the sunshine. They were left in
total darkness.

Then Matt heard a scraping noise and a
match spurted into flame. Chang's face was
illuminated, looking like a golden mask
suspended in the darkness.

'Follow me,' he instructed.

He led them into a narrow passage that
went off from the chamber. After a few paces
the match burned down. They continued
in the pitch-black, feeling their way along the
walls.

Then Chang struck another match. By its
light Matt saw a smooth metal chute, like a
giant enclosed slide. He looked down it, but
could see nothing but blackness.

'Follow me,' said Chang again.

He got on to the slide and blew out the

match. In the darkness they heard the sound of his body whooshing away down the chute, getting fainter and fainter until it died away. Matt thought that he heard a faint, distant thud at the bottom.

'Me next!' said Catarina. 'I love slides!' And away she went down the chute.

Shawn went next, then Olivier.

Left alone in the darkness, Matt felt his way to the lip of the chute. His heart was thumping fast. This was an amazing adventure, something he couldn't have dreamed of just a day ago. It was thrilling to be part of it. Yet it was scary too. Matt had never had a great head for heights and now he found he wasn't too keen on depths either.

Matt breathed deeply, hoisted himself on to the chute – and let go.

The descent felt almost vertical. Within a few seconds, he was falling very fast indeed.

It felt as if he'd left his stomach behind at the top. He forced himself to be calm. He made his muscles relax and simply lay on his back, letting gravity do the work. There was, after all, not much else he could do.

Then Matt felt the slope flattening out. He was slowing down. He hit the ground with a gentle bump, and stood up.

'So we have all arrived safely,' said Chang. It was a little lighter down here – there were a few dim lanterns on the walls and Matt saw that they were in a large, rocky chamber with a number of passages leading off from it.

'We still have some way to go,' said Chang. 'It will get darker again. Hold on to each other please. It would not do to get lost. This place is a labyrinth. You could wander around for the rest of your life and never find way out.'

They all linked hands and walked on with

Chang in the lead. They went into one of the passages.

Very soon, darkness descended. The air became stuffier. Matt sensed that the ceiling was low, only just above their heads.

The passage twisted and meandered. Every now and again Chang would turn off and lead them down another equally meandering passage. Matt took care to memorize the turnings they took as they went along – left, left, right, left, right, the middle passage of three . . .

Chang came to a stop at a junction. Dimly, Matt saw two passages leading away and knew that he'd seen them before.

Chang stood in thought. 'It is long time since I last came through these passages,' he said. 'I . . . I think it is to the left –'

'We've been this way before, sir,' said Matt. 'I remember it. We turned left last time, so . . .'

'Yes,' said Chang slowly. 'So this time we must take the right passage. Otherwise we will be going in circles. Well done, Matt. You have saved us. Now, I think, I know the way.'

'Nice work, Matt!' said Catarina.

They went on. The narrow escape from getting lost had unnerved Matt. *What a disaster it would be to lose our way*, he thought.

The darkness was beginning to get too much. At any moment, Matt felt, something unexpected might fly at him out of the dark. He found himself longing for light, in the same way you'd thirst for water in the desert.

The thumping of his heart accelerated. He was feeling seriously claustrophobic. He noticed a tension, a slight trembling in Shawn's arm – Shawn must be feeling it too. There was an atmosphere of barely suppressed panic. Matt could hear it in the quick, shallow breathing of the others. He was desperate to break out into a run – but where would he run to?

Out of the darkness came Chang's quiet, steady voice. 'Stay calm. Breathe deeply. Keep walking steadily, one foot in front of the other.'

Chang's words had an immediate calming effect. Matt found that if he concentrated on breathing, and on the rhythmic tread of his feet, the panic receded.

Then Matt saw a glimmer of light ahead. Relief flooded him. The light got brighter and larger. They came into a kind of ante-chamber cut into the rock, lit by yellow lanterns.

There was an ornate pagoda-style archway with Chinese characters written across the top. The archway was guarded by four men wearing black masks. They were big, muscular men, and each held a wooden staff. Matt's body tensed and he instinctively assumed a fighting stance. Beside him he saw the other

Tigers do the same. The guards looked like they meant business, but if the Tangshan Tigers had to fight their way past them, they were ready to try.

But to Matt's surprise the guards bowed and stepped back to let them pass. Of course – they must have been expecting Chang. The other six keyholders would be waiting beyond that arch. And somewhere, in one of these caves or chambers, they were keeping Li-Lian – hopefully still unharmed.

They passed through the arch and along a short corridor. At the end was a door. Chang turned the handle and pulled it open.

They found themselves in a huge, gleaming control room, so vast and hi-tech that Matt heard Shawn gasp in amazement at the sight of it. There were metal pipes running around the walls, a huge console with a bewildering array of dials, and several bleeping, winking devices

that Matt couldn't even begin to guess the
purpose of. There was a huge plasma screen
on the wall, showing an intricate network
of pipes, and a number of glowing red lights
moving slowly across it. In the centre of the
floor was a large silver square plate of metal,
about the size of a squash court. It looked like
it was covering something. Matt wondered
what lay beneath it.

Then Matt started. Next to the metal plate
was Li-Lian, tied to a chair. She was flanked
by six men in expensive-looking suits. Four
looked middle-aged, two younger; but all
bore the same expression of hard-faced
determination.

Li-Lian's face lit up at the sight of her
grandfather. She called out something in
Mandarin.

'Yes, Li-Lian!' said Chang. 'I am here – you
are safe now!'

Li-Lian looked at Matt and the Tangshan Tigers in surprise. She smiled. 'How pleasant to see you again! I did not expect to meet you here!'

'Yeah, well, we were in the area, so we thought we'd drop in,' said Catarina.

One of the men – grizzled and thickset, with a greater air of power and authority than the others – stepped forward and said something in Mandarin. He pointed at the Tangshan Tigers.

'They are my friends,' said Chang in English. 'They have come to help me bring Li-Lian home.'

'I do not know what help you think a group of children can provide,' replied the man, also in English. 'Nor why you should need help. All we want from you is the key. I hope for the girl's sake you have it.'

'Sang, I earnestly ask you to think carefully –'

'The key!' rapped out Sang. He thrust out his hand. 'Give us the key at once! We want, and we will have, what is ours by right!'

'You have no right to the oil.'

So that's what this is all about, Matt realized! Everyone knew the world's supplies of oil were running dry – Mr Jensen had been telling them about it in geography only last week. Oil was a commodity so precious that people were prepared to fight wars over it.

Sang gave a short, angry laugh. 'Might is right – do you know this English saying? I advise you to remember we hold all the cards. You see that all but one of the keys are in place.'

Matt followed his gaze and saw that the silver plate that was set into the floor had seven golden locks. From six of the locks, golden keys protruded.

And underneath, Matt realized, lay a glistening sea of black oil. Now he understood.

'Beneath our feet is enough oil to make us the richest men in the world,' said Sang, in a more reasonable, persuasive tone. 'You too, if you care to join us.'

Chang shook his head dismissively.

'That is your choice,' said Sang. 'But you will not prevent us taking what is ours. Hand over the key!'

'Reflect, Sang. Twenty years ago, you made promise to keep secret of this oil safe from world. If you break that promise, what do you think will happen? Oil companies will flock to this area – the Great Wall itself will be torn down to get at the oil. Is that what you want? To see our history destroyed?'

'Enough talking!' said Sang angrily.

He clapped his hands. One of the younger men picked up a sword and drew it from its sheath with a faint, metallic hiss. He went over to Li-Lian and pulled her head back by the hair, exposing her neck. He raised the sword; the blade gleamed under the fluorescent lights.

Matt gasped. He wasn't going to kill her in cold blood – was he?

Chapter 8

TIME TO FIGHT!

'No!' said Chang. 'I will give you key.'

He looked abject, defeated. Matt had
never seen him like this. Usually Chang stood
upright, his back straight, his head held high.
Now his shoulders drooped as he fumbled
in the leather case for the key. Matt saw the
other Tigers look as shocked as he felt. Was
their master defeated, then? Was there no
choice but to give in?

'I am glad you see sense,' said Sang. 'Of
course, you lose your share of the wealth,

because of the stubborn resistance you have
displayed.'

Chang bowed submissively. He held out the
key in the palm of his hand.

Sang drew himself up and shook his head.
'You will place the key in the lock yourself,'
he said. 'And you will turn it for us. And
then, perhaps, you will learn a lesson in
humility.'

Matt felt his cheeks burning in outrage.
How could anyone speak to Chang Sifu
like that? Chang walked slowly over to the
silver plate. Matt hated to see him doing as
he was told so meekly. He clenched his fists,
wishing there was something, anything, he
could do.

But, as he passed the Tangshan Tigers,
Chang turned his head ever so slightly and
said, in a scarcely audible undertone, 'Do you
think you're up to it?'

Matt felt a surge of adrenalin. He knew at once what they had to do. He saw the other Tangshan Tigers bracing themselves for action too. They all exchanged glances, and Matt gave a very slight nod.

Then, without any word or warning, Matt leapt forward and launched a high, powerful axe kick at the man with the sword.

Taken completely by surprise, the man had barely begun to react when Matt's foot struck his upper arm. The sword went clattering across the floor. The man cursed and threw a wild punch at Matt, which Matt dodged easily. But the man kept coming at him, yelling some sort of Chinese battle-cry. He'd clearly been trained in martial arts, and though not as quick as Matt, he was much bigger and stronger – Matt blocked, dodged and counter-punched, keeping him at bay but having to give ground.

Meanwhile, around Matt things were happening very fast. Out of the corner of his eye, Matt saw Chang take out one of the men with a single one-inch punch to the solar plexus. The man groaned and collapsed.

Olivier was engaged in furious combat with another of the men – they punched, kicked, blocked and dodged with bewildering speed. Olivier hadn't been able to take the man out yet, but was keeping him busy enough so that he couldn't get at the sword, or at Li-Lian.

'Quick!' called Li-Lian. 'Untie me!'

Shawn ran over and quickly got to work untying her bonds.

With shouts of protest, two of the men moved to stop him – but Catarina moved in between them and threw a series of high kicks. The men backed away, wary of her flying feet, looking for a chance to counter-attack. One of them managed to block one of her kicks and throw her off balance. Catarina cried out as she stumbled – but before either of the men could press home this advantage, Chang was there, his feet and fists a whirling blur. He downed one of the men with a high kick to the jaw. The other backed right off.

Matt felt a surge of pride to be fighting alongside such a master. But he still had his own opponent to worry about – the man was coming at him throwing punches, still yelling those bloodcurdling yells. Matt caught the man's outstretched arm and, using a judo throw he'd learned from a classmate back in England, sent the man flying over his back. The man crashed to the floor and lay there groaning.

And now Li-Lian was free. Her face came alive as she rushed to join in the fighting – and Matt could see by the expert way she feinted and punched and threw kung fu kicks that her grandfather had taught her well. So that made five of them, plus Chang, who was easily worth three men, against the three keyholders who were still standing. It looked to be almost over.

But now Sang took up the fight. Until this point he had stood back from the fight; suddenly he snatched up the fallen sword. Matt saw at once that he was an expert swordsman. He whirled the sword around in front of him, carving lightning-fast patterns in the air, hissing through his teeth like an angry snake. They all backed away from him, even Chang.

Sang let out a loud shout. A moment later, the four masked, muscular guards from outside rushed in.

Now the odds didn't look so good. It was six against seven – and four of the seven were armed. And now the three men who had been felled earlier were getting back on their feet.

Without Li-Lian and the Tangshan Tigers, even Chang wouldn't have stood a chance.

The guards piled into the fight, swinging and thrusting their staffs. One of them aimed a vicious blow at Matt, which would have taken his head off if it had connected. Matt ducked, and felt the wind of the staff whistling past his scalp. At the same time, he instinctively countered with a snap-kick to the guard's knee. The man stumbled and fell.

The other Tangshan Tigers were fighting for all they were worth, just staying out of reach of the flailing staffs, getting in counter-blows when they could, shouting warnings to each other.

'Look out!' shouted Li-Lian, and just in time Catarina jumped back from a strike aimed at the side of her head. She whirled round and counter-attacked with a spear-hand thrust to her attacker's midriff, which doubled him up, leaving him choking for breath.

But it was a desperate rearguard action. The guards knew what they were doing with those staffs, and it took all the Tangshan Tigers' skill to avoid serious injury.

Sang was trying his best to cut Chang in half with the sword. Chang calmly avoided his vicious strokes, moving swiftly but without apparent effort. Then, after Sang had just missed with a particularly energetic swipe, Chang delivered a high kick that seemed to come out of nowhere. It caught Sang squarely on the jaw and Sang fell backwards, dropping the sword.

Now they had a much better chance. But with the fight still in the balance, Matt was amazed to see Chang scramble over to the silver plate and insert the golden key. He could hardly believe his eyes. Was Chang giving in, abandoning the battle when it was still undecided?

But then Chang did an unexpected thing. He turned the key clockwise, not anti-clockwise.

There was a click. A loud throbbing noise instantly started up, as if some powerful machinery had been set in motion.

For a moment, everyone froze. Sang was back on his feet, staring at Chang in anger and confusion.

'You fool!' he spat at Chang. 'What have you done?'

Matt looked up and saw something he couldn't believe at first. Then he did believe it, and his blood ran cold.

Slowly, steadily, the ceiling was descending.

Chang Sifu fixed Sang with a level gaze. 'It is you who are the fool,' he said. 'Did you think our superiors were unable to see what greed might drive men to? Now the oil is beyond reach, forever!'

He reached out and took Li-Lian's hand. Then he turned to the Tangshan Tigers. 'Quick – it is time to run!'

The Tangshan Tigers didn't need telling twice. They ran out of the control room and raced down the corridor. Behind, Matt heard the hoarse cries of the men they'd left behind – they were shouting to each other, but Matt couldn't understand what they were saying. Why didn't they run? Then the shouts stopped. What had happened?

Matt could still hear the relentless grinding overhead – it wasn't just the ceiling of the control room but the roof of the whole cave-system that was coming down. Several million tons of rock were slowly falling towards them.

'If we don't get out in time, we'll be crushed to a paste!' said Shawn.

'We'd kind of figured that out, Shawn,' said Catarina.

They ran through the dark labyrinthine corridors, following Chang, keeping close together. The roof was still remorselessly descending.

As they ran, a thought kept troubling Matt. How were they ever going to climb up that smooth, nearly vertical chute to get to safety? It just wasn't possible!

At last the dim lights of the entry chamber shone ahead of them. They'd made it! The roof was barely a metre above their heads now. Matt felt weak with relief. He saw that next to the chute was a hole in the roof, like a chimney, and dangling from it was a rope.

'So that's how they get in and out!' said Matt.

'Yes,' said Chang. 'Slide down chute, climb up rope. Which is what we now must do, and quickly! Li-Lian, you go first.'

Li-Lian moved towards the rope – then stopped.

For the second time that day, Matt's blood ran cold. The rope was disappearing. It was slithering up the chimney like a snake escaping into a hole.

Chang was the quickest to react. He flung himself forward and made a grab for the rope. His fingertips just grazed the end of it.

Then it was gone.

'But how –?' said Matt.

'They must have taken secret short cut,' said Chang. 'This place is full of passages.'

High, high above was a small circle of light. Sang's head appeared in it, looking down on them with an angry smile.

'Farewell, Chang,' he said. 'You have cost

us untold riches – and your reward is that you must remain trapped here with your granddaughter. How thoughtful to bring your friends along as well!'

TRAPPED

The roof had sunk to barely a hand's-breadth above their heads. Soon they would have to stoop. Then bend double. And then . . .

'There must be some way out!' said Matt.

'Can't we climb the chute?' said Olivier.

'Not possible,' said Chang. 'Too smooth and too steep. It was designed to be so.'

'Then what about the chimney where the rope was? Can't we climb that?' said Catarina.

'It is as smooth as the chute. And steeper,' said Chang.

'But we could stand in it – then the roof wouldn't –' began Shawn.

'There is room for only three of us to stand at the bottom,' said Chang quietly. His brow wrinkled in thought.

Matt felt a shiver run up his spine. Did that mean of the six of them just three could be saved? But they'd have to stand there, helpless, while their three comrades were crushed to a paste. And they wouldn't be saved anyway. They'd simply be stuck at the bottom of the chimney with no chance of rescue. They'd die just as surely. It would take a few days longer, that was all.

But there must be some way, he thought furiously . . .

'Wait,' said Li–Lian's small, clear voice in the gloom. She seemed perfectly calm and serene. 'I can see the end of the rope at the top of the chimney. Perhaps . . .

'Yes? What is it?' said Chang. 'Speak quickly, child.'

'If we make a chain – a human chain –'

'What do you mean?' asked Shawn.

'Stand on each other's shoulders – then the person at the top might reach rope.'

Hope flared in Matt's heart. Yes, it was possible . . . Possible, but fiendishly difficult. He remembered how they'd struggled and failed to form a human pyramid in the training session – was it only yesterday? But this time there was no room for failure. He'd have to focus. Concentrate. Shut out the distraction of that hideous grinding noise. He'd have to get his mind and body working in perfect harmony.

They all would.

'We must act swiftly,' said Chang. His voice was calm. 'I will stand at base.'

'OK – I'll go on your shoulders,' said Matt.

Chang looked serious. 'You will be bearing

much weight – do you think you can manage it?'

'Yes,' said Matt. His mouth was dry.

'I'd better go next,' said Olivier.

'Then me,' said Shawn.

'And then me,' said Catarina.

'And I will go last, because I am the lightest of all!' said Li-Lian.

Master Chang stood, legs wide, positioning himself in the centre of the chimney. 'Ready, Matt?'

Chang held out his two hands, fingers linked together, creating a foothold for Matt. Matt hoisted himself up and stood, swaying, on Chang's shoulders. He forced himself to breathe deeply, calming himself. Into his mind there floated an image of a lotus flower. He focused on it, centring his thoughts there rather than on his fear. It worked. He felt calmed, refreshed.

Now he stood firm and steady. 'OK, Olivier – go!'

Matt put out his hands to help Olivier, as Chang had done for him. Olivier scrambled up, putting a kneecap into Matt's face by accident – but Matt stood firm, keeping his balance.

Slowly, cautiously, Olivier stood up on Matt's shoulders. 'All right, Shawn – I'm ready!'

Again, Matt used his hands to help Shawn up and adjusted to the changed balance. He had the combined weight of two boys pressing down on his shoulders now. It was hard. And it was getting hot in the crowded chimney. Matt felt sweat trickling down his face and between his shoulder blades.

But he stood firm. They'd come so far – they couldn't fail, they couldn't let Chang down now! If he could just hold it for another minute . . .

Now the agile Catarina was climbing up.
She made it to the top without mishap. But
the added weight and the shift in balance was
bad news for Matt. He swayed and staggered,
feeling the others above struggling for their
balance too. He put out his hand and touched
the side of the chimney. That steadied him for
a moment. But he couldn't lean against the
side for too long – he had to keep vertical to
bear the weight above him, otherwise it would
pull him off Chang's shoulders and they'd all
come crashing down.

With a supreme effort, Matt pushed off
from the wall so that he was standing vertically
again, and held it. At once it felt easier. Now
the weight was transmitted through the whole
length of his body.

'I am nearly there!' called Catarina. 'Is
everyone all right?'

'Fine,' said Shawn.

'Never . . . better . . .' Olivier added.

Matt didn't waste energy speaking.

'Li-Lian, you are ready?' called Catarina.

'Coming!'

Li-Lian climbed nimbly up the chain. A few agonizing moments later Matt heard her call out: 'Done it! I'm out!'

The human chain swayed again, dangerously.

'Watch out!' Catarina screamed. 'I'm going to . . .'

She tumbled down, grabbing at the others to break her fall. The chain broke up. They collapsed to the ground – Matt was pushed aside by the tumbling bodies and rolled under the descending roof.

It felt to Matt as though the ground had rushed up and hit him. He was winded, and he had bitten his tongue – he felt the blood running down his chin, although, strangely, no pain. He tried to get up, but bumped his head

on the rocky roof, still pitilessly descending.
He stayed on his hands and knees. It was pitch-
dark; the lanterns had been extinguished.

'Everyone all right?' came Chang's voice. He
was crouched next to Matt, under the roof.

'All right so far,' came Shawn's voice,
sounding shaky.

'We're OK,' said Catarina.

'But what about you?' said Olivier.

The three of them were safe, for the time
being, in the chimney. But there was no room
for Matt or Chang to take refuge there. Matt
hoped the rope descended soon. Why wasn't it
coming down?

What if – a dreadful thought struck Matt
*– what if the villains were waiting at the top and
had grabbed Li-Lian as she emerged? Then the rope
would never reappear, and –*

'Here comes the rope!' called Li-Lian.

Matt heard the rope come snaking down.

Catarina grabbed hold and shinned her way up, fast.

Chang pushed Matt. 'There is room for you in hole now. Go!'

'But what about you?'

'Just go!'

Chang pushed him again and Matt rolled into the chimney. He stood up, pressed against Shawn and Olivier. 'Quick!' he said to Shawn. 'Climb up, or Chang will be –'

Shawn didn't need to be told twice. He swarmed up the rope.

Matt and Olivier knelt and reached out to help Chang into the chimney. Not before time. The rock was already beginning to press down on him as they caught his hands and hauled him to safety.

Olivier climbed up next.

Then Matt. He felt as if he had no strength left in his body. His limbs were heavy and aching; he couldn't breathe in enough oxygen to keep him going. The taste of blood was in his mouth.

The rope seemed to go on for ever. *I'll never make it*, he thought – and suddenly he felt the rope slipping through his fingers, burning his hands as he slid down.

He tightened his grip again involuntarily. He hung there, swaying, trying to breathe deeply.

'Come on, Matt!' he heard Li-Lian call. 'You can do it!'

Her voice gave Matt courage. *Yes*, he thought grimly. *I can. I can do it.*

He started climbing again, slowly, painfully. Hand over hand, hand over hand . . . A few metres more . . .

And then Li-Lian and Shawn were grabbing his arms, pulling him up the last little bit, dragging him out to safety.

He found himself in the same space they'd used to enter and flopped on to his back, panting, grateful to be alive.

And finally Chang emerged.

They came out, blinking, into the daylight.

Carl, still waiting by the wall, stared at them in shock. Matt glanced around at the others and for a moment saw them through Carl's eyes: pale, weary, with dirt-streaked faces; Olivier had a bruise on his cheek, Catarina's hand was bleeding and there was blood around Matt's mouth. They must have looked like a crowd of zombies.

'What's happened to you? What's been going on? What was that horrible rumbling noise?' said Carl. 'I've been going out of my mind here!'

The sound of the roof descending must have been heard up here, Matt realized. Looking up at the top of the wall, he saw the tourists were running, piling into their coaches. Someone had got hold of a megaphone and was urging the stragglers on.

'Exit the area as quickly as possible. Keep calm but keep moving! Everyone exit the area as quickly as possible!'

They must have thought an earthquake was coming.

'I didn't know what to do!' said Carl. 'I thought the whole place was going to collapse or blow up! It's not fair, leaving me here on my own!'

Chang was the last to emerge from the hole in the wall. He shut the sliding panel behind him with his usual care and precision. Then he pulled Li–Lian to him and hugged her, stroking her hair, murmuring to her in Mandarin.

'Hello?' said Carl. 'Will someone please tell

me what's going on? I've been stuck out here, on my own; I thought there was an earthquake. And who's this girl?'

Chang Sifu straightened up and looked Carl squarely in the eye.

'Can you keep a secret, Carl?'

For a moment, Matt wondered if the narrow escape in the caves below had unhinged Chang's mind. Could blabbermouth Carl keep a secret? That was like asking a tortoise if it could do the high jump, or a flea if it could keep still.

'Sure, I can keep a secret!' said Carl, his curiosity evidently aroused. 'What is it?'

'Never speak of what you have seen today. Forget that you saw us go under the Great Wall – forget you saw us come out with Li-Lian. Forget everything that has happened since you left school yesterday.'

'OK,' said Carl. 'But what's the secret?'

'That is the secret.'

'But what happened in there? Five minutes ago a bunch of Chinese guys came running out – who were they?'

'This part of the secret it is not necessary for you to know. You need only keep silent about what you have seen.'

'But that's not fair!' protested Carl. 'These guys know all about it, and you're leaving me out –'

'If you are able to keep silent, I can give you an alibi for being absent from school premises,' said Chang mildly. 'But if not – well, I cannot be held responsible for what Mr Wu might do.'

'But I . . . but I . . .' Carl spluttered, his face growing red. Matt had to bite his lip to stop himself from laughing.

Then he thought of something that made it seem less funny. The Tangshan Tigers were going to need an alibi every bit as much as

Carl would. Despite Shawn's clever trick with the cyber roll-call device, their absence must have been discovered by now. They had been away a whole night and the best part of the next day.

'What are we going to do, sir?' asked Matt. 'What can we tell Mr Wu?'

'Ah – did I not mention? Just before I left, I wrote a note for Mr Wu, saying I had organized training trip for some pupils. Your name was not on note, Carl, but I can tell Mr Wu this was accidental omission. If you are able to keep secret. Yes?'

Carl nodded sulkily. There wasn't much else he could do.

'But wait a minute!' said Catarina. 'How did you know to leave the note?'

'I anticipated possibility that some students might try to help,' said Chang.

The Tangshan Tigers exchanged glances and

laughed. Was there anything that Chang Sifu
did not know?

'It is too late to return to Academy tonight,'
said Chang. 'The journey is long and we are all
tired. I know a boarding house in Huanghua
where the food is very good. We will rest
tonight, and travel back tomorrow.'

Rest and food! Matt couldn't decide which
he wanted more right now. As they walked
back to the town, he thought about everything
that had happened in the space of a single day.
They had saved Li-Lian's life – which, after all,
was the whole purpose of the mission. And in
return she had saved theirs.

On the other hand, it had also been a bad
day. Six evil men – men who wouldn't hesitate
to kill – were walking free.

Chang Sifu fell into step with Matt and said
quietly: 'Do not worry, Matt. There will be
another chance.'

Matt looked up, confused. 'A chance?'

'A chance to bring those men to justice. And remember – we saved Li-Lian. And we saved Great Wall of China too! It is not every day one can say that.'

Matt turned to take one last look at the Great Wall. The rough stones glinted gold in the setting sun. It was a beautiful sight.

A wave of tiredness swept over him. The day's events had been exhausting. He was glad they weren't travelling home that night.

They reached the boarding house a few minutes later. It was a traditional Chinese building by the roadside, with paper lanterns hanging outside.

Lost in his thoughts, Matt lagged behind. Chang, Li-Lian and the Tangshan Tigers were already going in. But he wasn't the last. Carl was bringing up the rear, scuffing his shoes in the dust, muttering sullenly to himself. It occurred to Matt that Carl was going to be a problem in the future. He knew enough to make him curious, and was resentful about being kept out of the secret. He would make trouble for the Tangshan Tigers if he could . . .

Well, that was another problem for another day. Matt shook himself, and ran to catch up with his friends.

'Hey, here he is!' said Olivier.

'You did good, Matt!' said Catarina.

'We all did!' said Matt. 'It was a team effort!'

'A team effort by the Tangshan Tigers!' said Shawn.

'What is this?' asked Li-Lian. 'The Tangshan Tigers?' Matt and his friends smiled at each other.

'Oh, just an idea I had,' said Matt.

'A good one,' added Catarina. Matt couldn't believe that when he'd arrived in Beijing he hadn't even met Catarina, Shawn and Olivier. And now they had another friend – Li-Lian. The Tangshan Tigers were a tighter unit than ever before. Who knew what they'd take on next?

Masters of Martial Arts
Fighters of Crime
together they're the

TANGSHAN TIGERS

Matt

Shawn

Catarina

puffin.co.uk

Olivier

TANGSHAN TIGERS

Catarina Ribeiro

Age: 12

Nationality: Brazilian

Sport: Capoeira

Special skill: Agility

Strengths: Extremely graceful, so capoeira is the perfect sport for her. Feisty and spirited, her personality means she is always ready for a challenge.

Weaknesses: As a crime-fighter, she needs to learn to follow her head rather than her instinct. She also has a rebellious streak that could get her into trouble.

Join the Team and Win a Prize!

Do YOU have what it takes to be a Tangshan Tiger?

Answer the questions below for the chance to win an exclusive Tangshan Tigers kit bag. Kit bag contains T-shirt, headband and cloth badge.*

1. What is the Chinese term for 'training hall'?

   a) Kwoon   **b)** Karateka   **c)** Kufu

2. Catarina's specialty is capoeira. Which country does this martial art come from?

   a) Britain   **b)** Bolivia   **c)** Brazil

3. In Karate, a sequence of movements performed without a partner is called kata.

   a) True   **b)** False

Send your answers in to us with your name, date of birth and address. Each month we will put every correct answer in a draw and pick out one lucky winner.

Tangshan Tigers Competition, Puffin Marketing, 80 Strand, London WC2R 0RL

Closing date is 31 August 2010.

Open to UK residents aged 6 or over. If you are under 13 you will need to include written permission from your parent or guardian

For full terms and conditions visit puffin.co.uk. Promoter is Penguin Books Limited. No purchase necessary

*subject to change